W9-CZV-752

YOU ARE AMAZING

BY
TY ALLAN JACKSON

please
read
to me

Dedicated to my AMAZING children
Aja, Ajayi, Alia

www.bigheadbooks.com

All rights reserved.

No part of this publication may be reproduced or transmitted in an form or by any means, electronic, mechanical, photocopying, recording, or otherwise, without prior written permission of Big Head Books.

Library of Congress Number: 2015906755

ISBN-10: 0692436383
ISBN-13: 978-0-692-43638-7

Copyright © 2015 Tyrone Allan Jackson

Printed in the U.S.A.

HOW TO USE THIS BOOK

YOU ARE AMAZING / I AM AMAZING is a dual purpose book.
On the YOU ARE AMAZING side YOU (the reader) will read this to a child.
Reading this will emphasize to the child how AMAZING they are.
At the end of the story the child can enter their name,
picture and list some of the things that make them AMAZING.
When the child is capable of reading to themselves they can
turn the book over and read I AM AMAZING,
affirming to themselves that they are AMAZING!

Feel free to post comments about the book on
the YOU ARE AMAZING / I AM AMAZING Facebook page
and/or www.bigheadbooks.com in the comments section.

Other books by Ty Allan Jackson

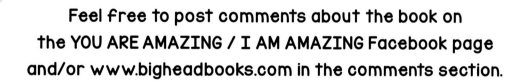

FOR AGES 0-6	**FOR AGES 6-10**	**FOR CHILDREN OF ALL AGES**
Shows children the power of imagination.	A classic good vs. evil superhero story.	Teaches finance and entrepreneurship.

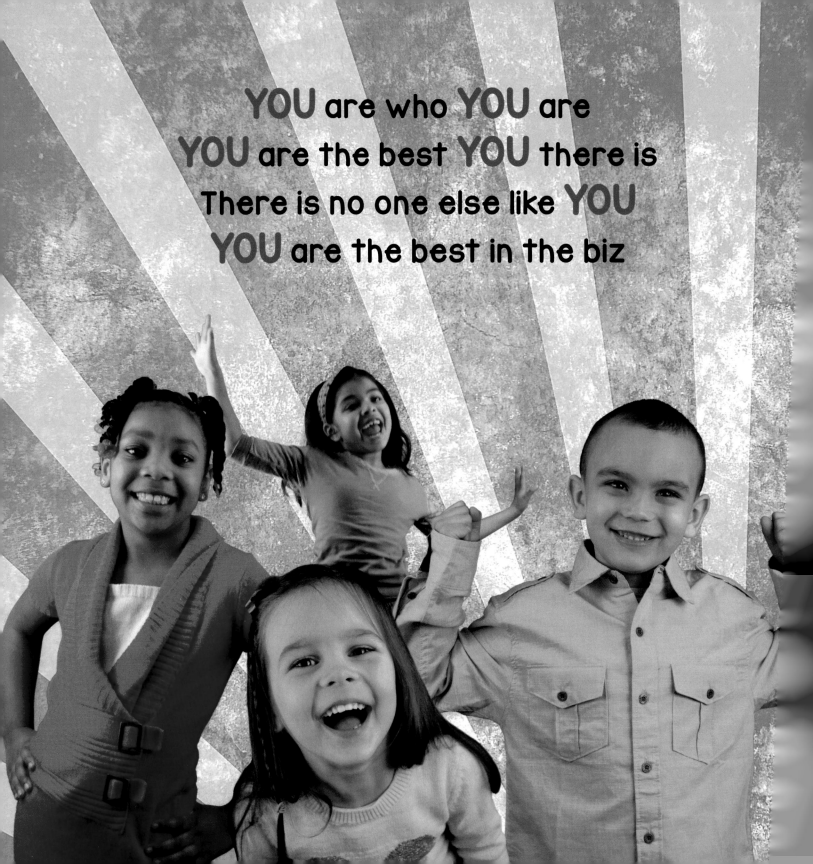

YOU are who YOU are
YOU are the best YOU there is
There is no one else like YOU
YOU are the best in the biz

Out of everyone in the world
Whether YOU are an adult or a kid
YOU are one of a kind
YOU are the best YOU there is

YOU are a beautiful human
YOU are a wonderful soul
YOU can do anything **YOU** wish
No matter the goal

When the going gets tough
YOU don't lose control
YOU give it your all
With your heart and your soul

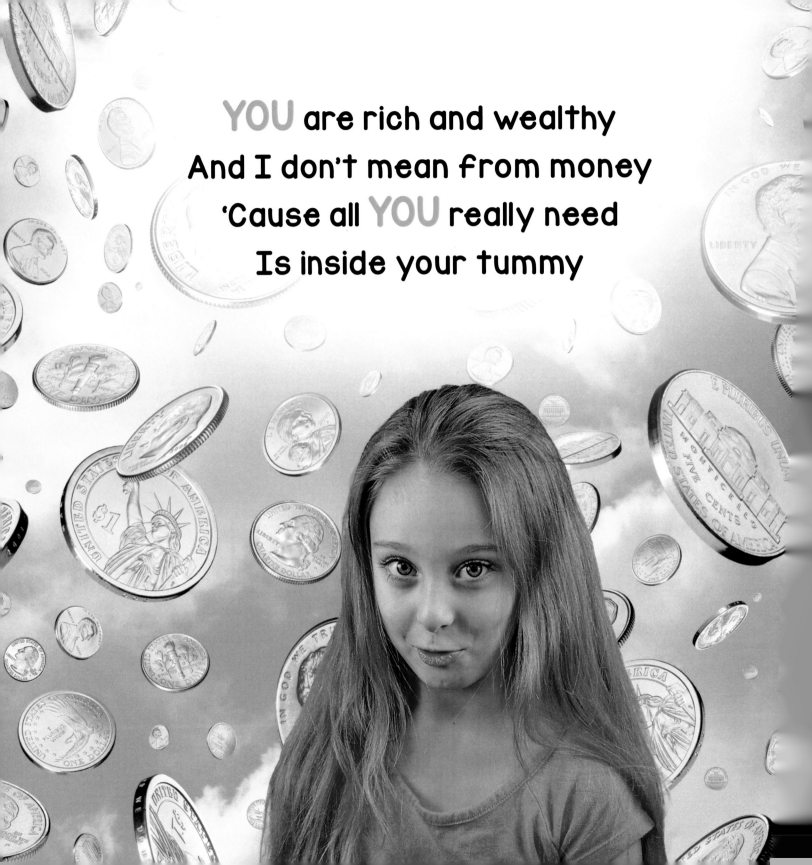

YOU are rich and wealthy
And I don't mean from money
'Cause all YOU really need
Is inside your tummy

The most important things are what YOU feel inside

That make YOU smile and give YOU butterflies

Like hugs
And kisses
And warm apple pies
Like puppies
And stars
And roller coaster rides

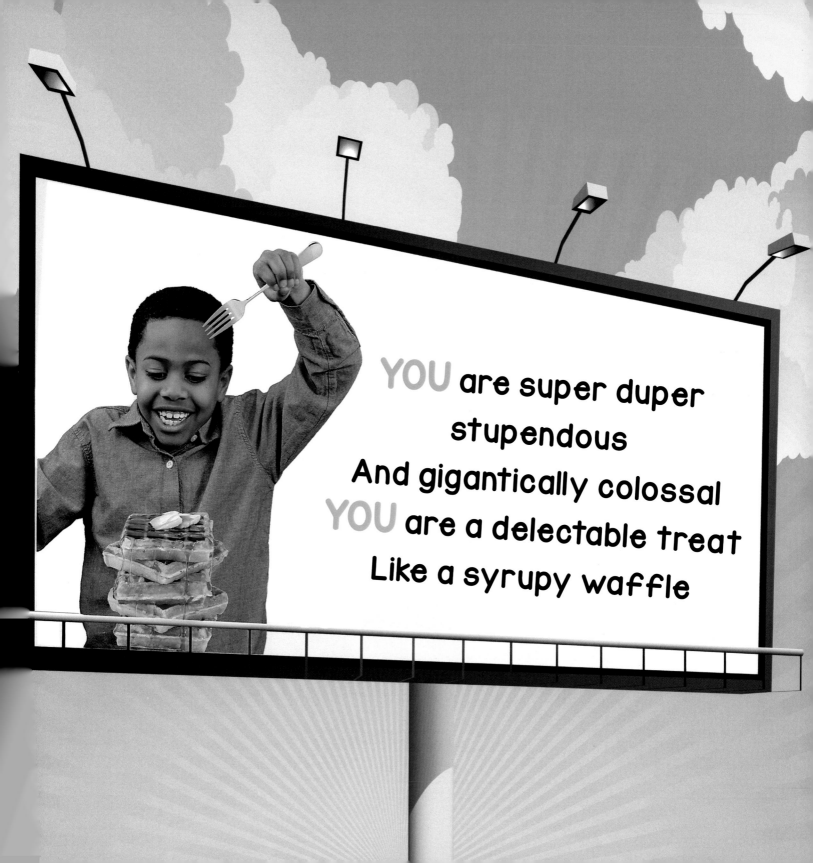

YOU are clever and bright and oh so astute
YOU are witty and brainy and very acute
Your smarts set YOU apart from all of your peers
YOU have the world's smartest computer
right between your ears

ASTUTE = KEEN OR SHARP

ABC

2×2=4

FUN

ACUTE = SMAR

YOU are a cool cucumber
Who is calm and collected
YOU are a smooth kinda dude
Who is highly respected
When things go wrong YOU don't get affected
YOU deal with the problem until it's corrected

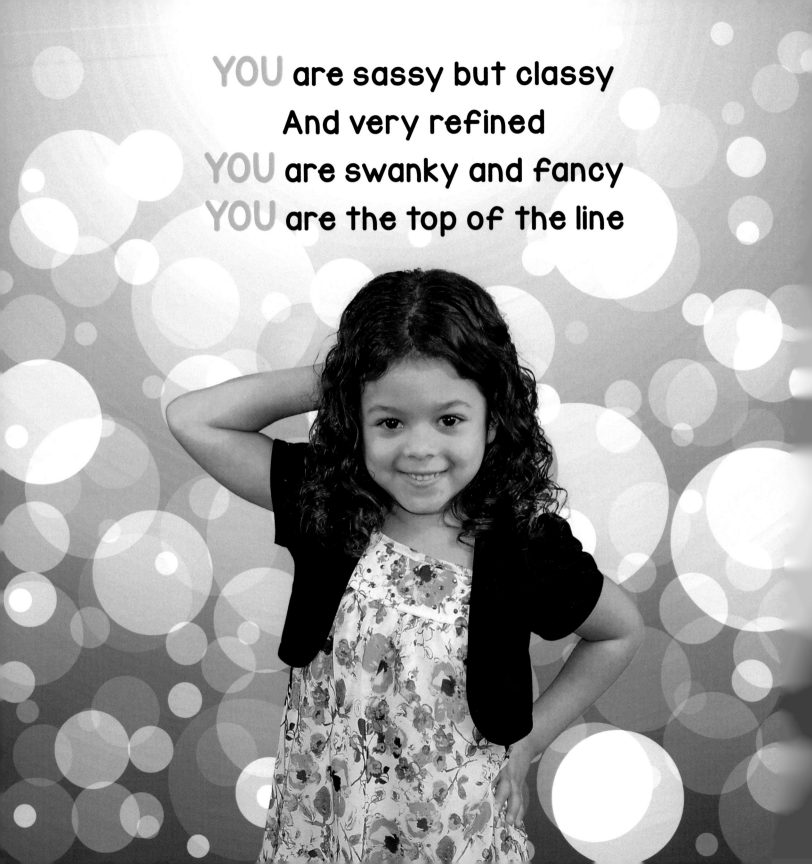

YOU are sassy but classy
And very refined
YOU are swanky and fancy
YOU are the top of the line

When it's your time to show
The world how **YOU** shine
YOU don't disappoint
YOU are one of a kind

YOU are amazingly amazing in every single way
From when the moon says goodbye
Until the sun fades away

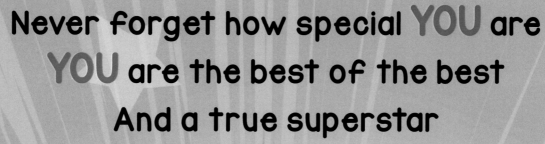

Never forget how special YOU are
YOU are the best of the best
And a true superstar

But in case YOU forget
How wonderful YOU are
I have two special rules
To make YOU go far

RULE #1

YOU
are
always
AMAZING!

RULE #2

When YOU don't feel amazing SEE RULE #1

My name is

_____

And I am AMAZING!

Place

Your Photo

Here

Sweet Kind Creative Respectful

Smart

I am AMAZING because

I am _____

Polite

I am _____

Funny

I am _____

Silly

I am _____

aring

Awesome   Playful   Curious

Happy

weet Kind Creative Respectful

Smart

I am AMAZING because

I am _____

I am _____

olite

Funny

I am _____

Silly

I am _____

Caring

Awesome Playful Curious

Happy

My name is

_____

And I am AMAZING!

Place
Your Photo
Here

RULE # 2

When I
don't
feel amazing
SEE
RULE
#1

RULE #1

I
am
always

AMAZING!

But in case I forget
How wonderful I am
I have two special rules
to remind me again

I will never forget how special I am
On the awesomely awesome meter
I am surely a 10

I am amazingly amazing
in every single way
From when the moon
says goodbye
Until the sun fades away

When it's my time to show
The world how **I** shine
I don't disappoint
I am one of a kind

I am sassy but classy
and very refined
I am swanky and fancy
I am the top of the line

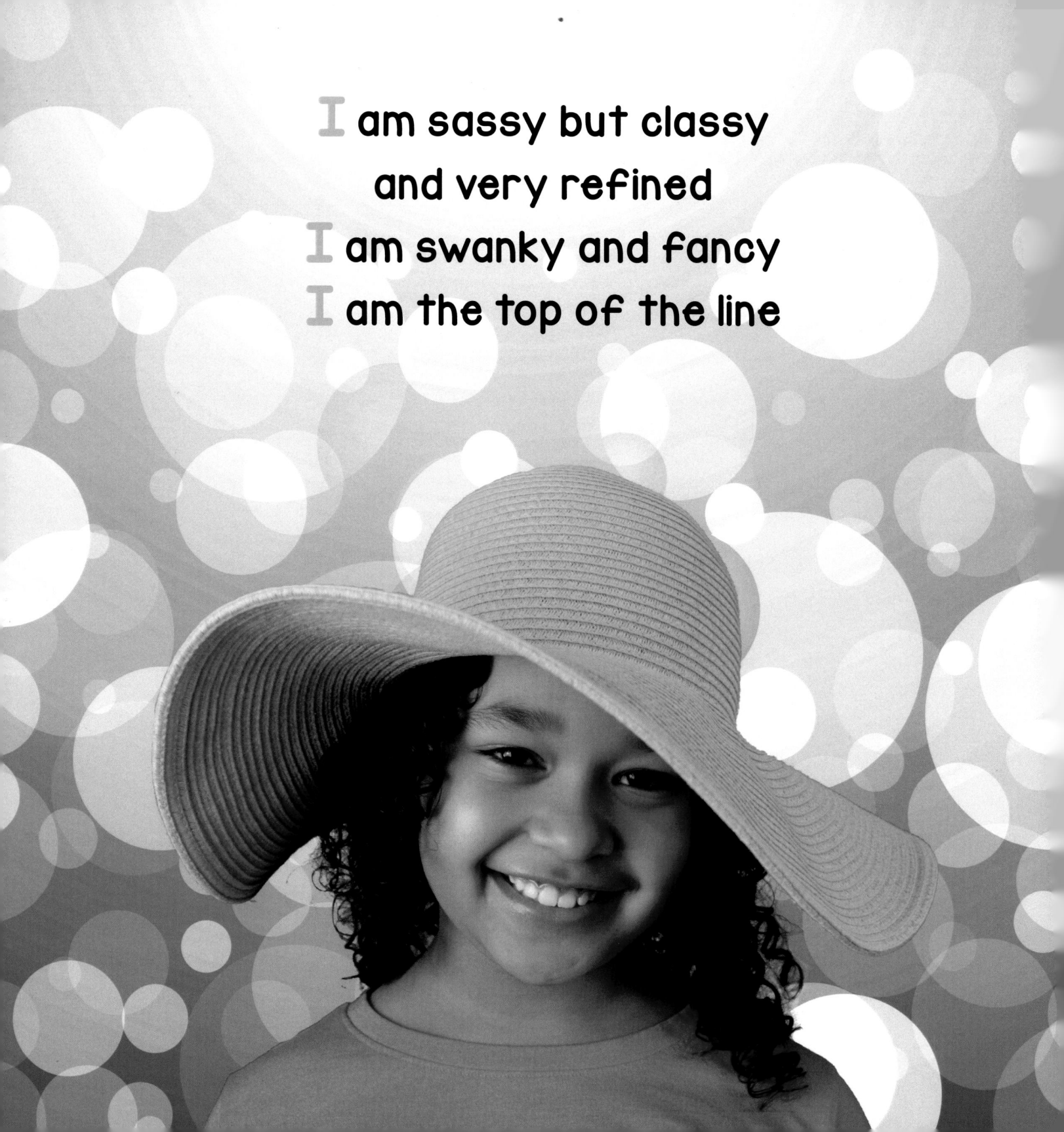

I am a cool cucumber
Who is calm and collected
I am a smooth kinda dude
Who is highly respected
When things go wrong I don't get affected
I deal with the problem until it's corrected

I am clever and bright and oh so astute
I am witty and brainy and very acute
My smarts set **ME** apart from all of my peers
I have the world's smartest computer
right between my ears

ASTUTE = KEEN
OR SHARP

ABC

2×2=4

FUN

ACUTE = SMART

Like hugs
And kisses
And warm apple pies
Like puppies
And stars
And roller coaster rides

The most
important thing
Is what
I feel inside

That makes
ME smile
and gives
ME butterflies

I am rich and wealthy
And I don't mean from money
'Cause all I really need
Is inside my tummy

When the going gets tough
I don't lose control
I give it my all
With my heart and my soul.

I am a beautiful human
I am a wonderful soul
I can do anything I wish
No matter the goal

Out of everyone in the world
And all the millions of kids
I am one of a kind
I am the best ME there is

I AM
AMAZING

BY
TY ALLAN JACKSON

I can
read by
myself

The Big Head Books Crew of Ty Allan Jackson, Martique Jackson, Eddie Taylor and Kathleen Garvey would like to give a whole lot of LOVE to:

Diane Jamison, Earl Taylor, Bob Sykes, Dr. Jason McCandless, John Bissell, Andrew Gagnon, Denise Mediavilla, David Cornellier, Judy Olds, Jolene Bull, Manzo Jackson, James Jackson Jr., Sheriff Tom Bowler, Jack Quinn, Al Bianchi, Ruth Taylor and all the beautiful children that participated in this project.

You are all AMAZING!

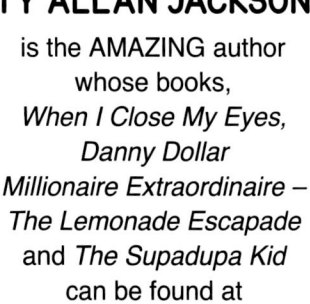

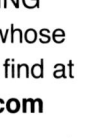

EDDIE TAYLOR
is the AMAZING photographer whose talents you can find at **edifyphoto.com**

TY ALLAN JACKSON
is the AMAZING author whose books, *When I Close My Eyes, Danny Dollar Millionaire Extraordinaire – The Lemonade Escapade* and *The Supadupa Kid* can be found at **bigheadbooks.com**

JOLENE BULL
is the AMAZING graphic designer and you can learn more about at **InTouchPrinting.com**

HOW TO USE THIS BOOK

YOU ARE AMAZING / I AM AMAZING is a dual purpose book.
On the I AM AMAZING side a child will read this to
themselves affirming that they are AMAZING.
At the end of the story the child can enter their name,
picture and list some of the things that make them AMAZING.
For younger children YOU (the reader) can turn the book over
and read YOU ARE AMAZING to the child,
emphasizing how AMAZING they are.

Feel free to post comments about the book on
the YOU ARE AMAZING / I AM AMAZING Facebook page
and/or www.bigheadbooks.com in the comments section.

Other books by Ty Allan Jackson

FOR AGES 0-6	**FOR AGES 6-10**	**FOR CHILDREN OF ALL AGES**
Shows children the power of imagination.	A classic good vs. evil superhero story.	Teaches finance and entrepreneurship.

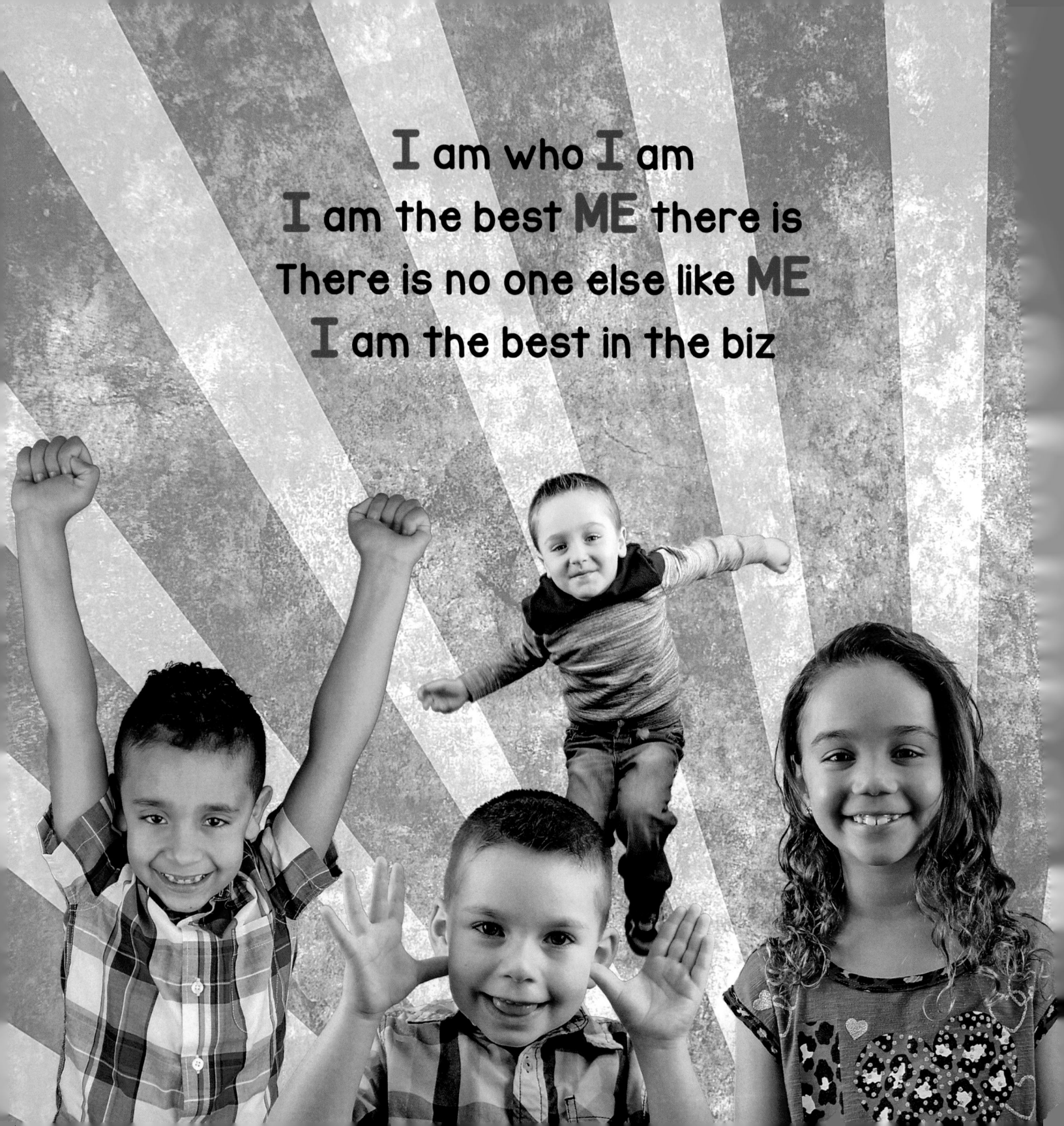

I am who I am
I am the best ME there is
There is no one else like ME
I am the best in the biz